THE
PURPLE
COAT

AMY HEST

pictures by

AMY SCHWARTZ

FOUR WINDS PRESS · NEW YORK

Four Winds Press
Macmillan Publishing Company
866 Third Avenue, New York, NY 10022
Collier Macmillan Canada, Inc.
Printed and bound in Japan
First American Edition
10 9 8 7 6 5 4 3 2 1
The text of this book is set in 16 pt. Cochin.
The illustrations are rendered in pencil
and watercolor and reproduced in full color.
Library of Congress Cataloging-in-Publication Data
Hest, Amy. The purple coat.
Summary: Despite her mother's reminder that "navy
blue is what you always get," Gabby begs her tailor
grandfather to make her a beautiful purple fall coat.
[1. Coats—Fiction. 2. Grandfathers—Fiction]
I. Schwartz, Amy, ill. II. Title.
PZ7.H4375Pu 1986   [E]   85-29186
ISBN 0-02-743640-3

For

JESSICA,

who also had to settle

for a plain blue coat

—A.H.

For

MARGE

—A.S.

Every fall, when the leaves start melting into pretty
purples and reds and those bright golden shades
of pumpkin, Mama says, "Coat time, Gabrielle!"

And they ride two trains to Grampa's tailor
shop in the city. On the Silver Express from
Meadowlawn to Pennsylvania Station, Gabby sits
close to the window, her nose pressed to the
smudge-glass for nearly an hour.

A lady in fur steps out on twenty-four, and
Gabby bends forward to pull her gray ragg socks
just past her knee. "I think a purple coat would be
much nicer," she answers.

"Purple?" Mama laughs.

"What's funny about purple?" demands Gabby,
puffing out her lower lip.

"There's nothing funny about it," admits Mama,
"but navy blue coats are what you always get."

Gabby makes a face. She sighs. She slips her left
foot into and out of the fringed moccasin that slides
off her heel when she walks.

"Greetings!" Grampa hugs them both in two woolly arms. He wears the same green sweater as always, with its suede-patched elbows and a line of

leather buttons down the front. Grampa calls it one of his treasures, a relic from the old days.

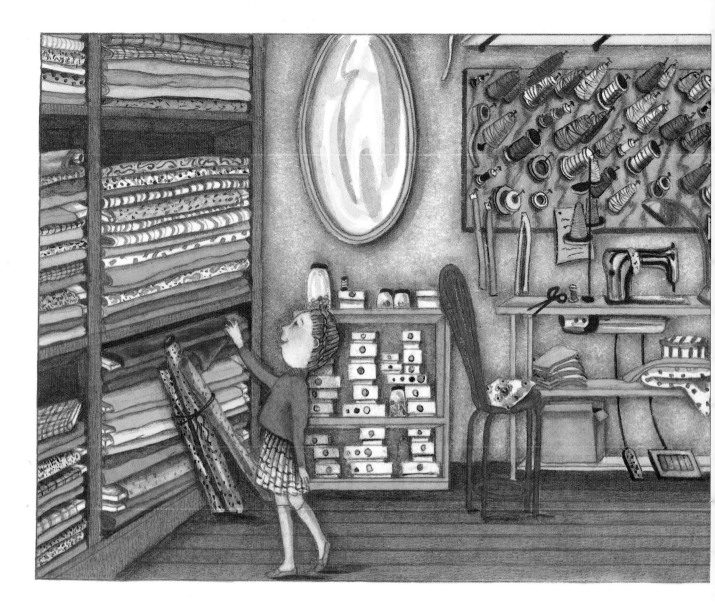

"Did we keep you waiting, Pop?" Mama stands at the wall of windows with city views all around.

Gabby moves toward the neat rows of fabric on the wall opposite. She drags red-painted fingertips, slowly, across the rainbow of colors stacked in open shelves way up to the ceiling and down to the polished wood floor. *Hello Purple*, she whispers,

When Grampa frowns, his thick eyebrows meet to cover up that tiny scar above his nose. "I suppose you asked your mother?"

Gabby looks at the toes of her moccasins.

"She said no purple coat," Grampa guesses.

"Not exactly," Gabby says slowly. "What she said was, navy blue coats are what I always get."

Grampa marches past the desk twice. Gabby marches behind. "Purple," he murmurs, and he seems to be talking to the air.

"A beautiful purple coat down to my ankles, with purple buttons and a big pocket on the side. It must have a purple hood," she goes on, "and a pleat in back to make it easy when I run. I'm a fast runner, Grampa."

He stops pacing and pours cream soda from a can. Bubbles rise quickly to the rim of two glasses. "A navy coat is such a classic, Gabrielle!"

"Once in a while it's good to try something new," she answers. "You said so yourself."

Grampa rubs a fist across the pointy part of his chin. He walks to the window with city views all around. Then he says, "Your mother wanted a tangerine-colored dress once, when she was six or so."

"Tangerine!" Gabby shrieks.

Grampa nods. "Tangerine, tangerine. All she talked about was tangerine!"

"Well, did you make her one? Did you, Grampa?"

"Finally, I did."

"I bet it was pretty too, almost as pretty as my purple coat could be."

Suddenly Grampa clicks two fingers in the air. "I have an idea," he begins. "Of course, one needs an exceptional tailor...."

"You're an exceptional tailor."

Grampa stands a little taller. "This year I will make you something very special," he announces, "a coat that is navy blue on one side—and purple on the other. Reversible!"

Gabby jumps high in the air. When she lands, her socks are scrunched around her ankles. "Let's make the purple side first."

He says it quietly.

"Different how?"

Gabby twirls until she's dizzy. She wishes she could race the elevator twenty-eight floors to the lobby. She would find her way to the Broadway Local, hide out in those underground tunnels.... "It's reversible!" she hears herself blurt out. "Navy on one side and purple on the other."

"Pop! Gabrielle gets a navy blue coat. Always," Mama adds firmly. "With two rows of buttons and a half belt in back."

"*You* wanted a tangerine dress once, when you were six or so."

Mama backs into the ancient wood chair with wheels on the bottom. She kicks off her pumps.

"Don't you remember? It had tangerine pockets and tangerine sleeves that puffed near the shoulders," Grampa says, "and tiny tangerine buttons…"

"…and a frilly tangerine collar!" Mama shakes her head. "It was so unlike *me* to want a dress like *that*!"

"Once in a while it's good to try something new. A person gets tired of the same old thing all the time," Gabby says. "Like salami."

"Or a navy blue coat?"

"It's such a pretty shade of purple, Mama. *Gorgeous!* You said so yourself."

Mama twists her mouth around.

"Remember tangerine!" Grampa points a finger in the air.

"Why do I feel outnumbered?" Mama sighs. Then she smiles, but very slowly. "I have a sneaky suspicion," she says at last, "this is going to be the best purple coat ever."

Gabby can't believe her ears. "You know, there just may be a day or two when I don't feel like purple." She says it softly, in her worried voice.

"There just may be," answers Mama. "So, on those days, Gabrielle, you can turn your sleeves inside out and flip your coat around to navy."